JOURNEY ACROSS PLANET X

D0011138

Welcome to the

STAR WARS®

Universe

Star Wars Journals

The Fight for Justice by Luke Skywalker

Hero for Hire by Han Solo

Captive to Evil by Princess Leia Organa

Star Wars Science Adventures

#1 Emergency in Escape Pod Four

#2 Journey Across Planet X

JOURNEY ACROSS PLANET X

Jude Watson and K.D. Burkett

SCHOLASTIC INC.
New York Toronto London Auckland Sydney
Mexico City New Delhi Hong Kong

ISBN 0-590-20228-6

12 11 10 9 8 7 6 5 4 3 2 1   9/9 0 1 2 3 4/0

Printed in the U.S.A.

First Scholastic printing, February 1999

Special thanks to Charles Doswell of the National Severe Storms Laboratory, Frank Heppner of the University of Rhode Island, Raoul Lopez of the National Severe Storms Laboratory, John Rojie of The Pennsylvania State University, David Rothstein of the University of Michigan, Mark Semon of Bates College, and Frank Summers of The American Museum of Natural History. Thanks also to SuperScience magazine for help with the Star Wars Science Activities.

JOURNEY ACROSS PLANET X

CRASH LANDING

The protocol droid See-Threepio peered out the viewport of the damaged escape pod. The long night was over, and a new day was beginning.

"It's getting light outside," he said, relieved. Then Threepio realized that it was time to exit the pod. Although the close quarters were cramped, he still preferred them to the perils that might lie on the unfamiliar planet.

"Actually, it's not *that* bright yet," he added quickly.

"Forget it, Threepio. I say we take off, pronto." This voice rose from the padded gee-couch, where twelve-year-old Stuart Zissu had been sleeping. Now he jumped up and began to buckle on his survival belt.

Astromech droid Artoo-Detoo let out a short whistle, then beeped.

"Review our situation first? I'd be happy to, Artoo," Threepio said. "We've crash-landed on a strange planet after being lost in space. The only thing we know for sure is that we're still in the Delantine system. The last message we received on the comlink was from Princess Leia, who told us to get to the nearest settlement to make contact with the Rebels. We have to do it within forty-eight hours or we'll be stranded, because the princess has ordered the evacuation of Rebel forces from all planets in the Delantine system. So we don't know where we are, where we're going, or who to contact, but we have to do it fast. In other words, we're doomed!"

Artoo gave a long warning whistle.

"I don't possibly see how I could be any more cheerful than I am," Threepio replied. "Considering that I'm lost, in terrible danger, and dented, to boot."

"If you don't stop complaining, I'll take a boot to *you,*" Stuart said, exasperated. "It's time for action, not whining!"

Everyone knew Stuart was anxious about his father. See-Threepio, Artoo-Detoo, and the research droid Forbee-X had been accompanying Governor Zissu and his young son to the planet Delantine when they'd been attacked by an Imperial warship. Governor Zissu had been captured, and the rest of them had just managed to escape in the pod.

Unfortunately, the controls of the pod had malfunctioned. They had barely made it through an asteroid field before crash-landing on the strange planet. They were certain that the pod had been sabotaged by a double agent back on the Rebel base at Yavin 4. Luckily, they were just able to get this information to the princess before all communication had been cut off.

"Now, now, everyone," Forbee-X spoke up. She wheeled forward from the corner. "Threepio is right — we should get moving. And Artoo is right, too. It's best to review our options before we start."

"I didn't say it was time to get moving," Threepio protested, waving his arms. "As a matter of fact, I think it might be best not to move at all. Maybe we should wait for the Rebels to find *us*."

Stuart ran his hands through his rumpled dark hair. "We know what we have to do," he said crisply. "We saw a city to the south as we were landing. So let's move!"

Forbee-X wheeled forward. The blue screen in her egg-shaped head flashed, then changed to a warm rose color. "Stuart, I know you're anxious to rescue your father. But the best thing we can do for him right now is be careful. If we start off in the wrong direction, we could waste precious time."

Stuart's freckled face flushed. "But we're wasting time now! We've already waited eight hours because you didn't want to travel while it was dark."

"And you needed rest," Forbee-X reminded him gently.

"But now we only have forty hours left!" Stuart exclaimed anxiously.

Artoo rolled toward Stuart. He gave a series of beeps and whirrs.

"Artoo doesn't want to waste any more time, either," Threepio translated. "But he thinks we should head for that river we glimpsed as we landed. It's to the east of us, so we should head in a southeasterly direction."

"East?" Stuart asked in disbelief. "But that will send us off course!"

"Artoo has a good point," Forbee-X said thoughtfully. "Settlements are usually built beside rivers, Stuart. It could be the most direct route."

"But what about the weather?" Threepio asked worriedly. "Yesterday, the temperature dropped alarmingly. The climate might be too cold for Master Stuart."

"The temperature dropped because the sun was setting," Stuart protested. "It was warm when we landed."

"But it could change at any time," Threepio reminded him. "Remember yesterday, when the leaves suddenly dropped off the trees all at once? This planet is strange, I tell you!"

"You're exaggerating!" Stuart exclaimed.

They both turned to the viewport. The sun shone on a blanket of fallen leaves outside.

"You see?" Stuart said. "Cool and clear. Perfect traveling weather."

But just as the words left his mouth, the sky turned dark gray.

Suddenly, it began to snow.

MAKING TRACKS

"You see!" Threepio cried triumphantly. "It's a blizzard! We can't possibly go out."

"It's not snowing that hard," Stuart protested.

Artoo beeped and whirred.

"I agree, Artoo," Forbee-X said. "Let's gather whatever supplies we can before we start."

Threepio wheeled to face Forbee-X. "Wait a minute. You understood Artoo!"

"I've been compiling bits of his vocabulary since the start of the journey," Forbee-X answered as she hooked a finger around a supply box and lifted the lid.

"I see," Threepio said. He felt a little jealous that Forbee-X could understand Artoo. Threepio had always been the one to interpret whatever his friend was saying. After all, Threepio was the droid with language skills. Did Forbee-X have to take the lead in *everything?*

Because the crash landing had scattered all the supplies, it took some time for Stuart and the droids to locate everything they would need and load it into transport packs.

Finally, they were done. "Do we have everything?" Forbee-X asked. "Condenser unit, glow rods, medpac, macrobinoculars? What about the fusion cutter?"

"Artoo took it and went outside," Threepio said. "He also said he was going to pack the parachute we used for the landing. He said it would make a good blanket for Stuart if the temperature drops at night."

Picking up the survival gear, Stuart, Forbee-X, and Threepio exited the pod. Outside, Artoo was busy using the fusion cutter to unscrew the bolts in the hull of the pod.

"Artoo, what are you doing?" Threepio asked. "We can't take the whole pod with us!"

Artoo loosened the last bolt. Then he pulled a curved sheet of metal off the frame of the pod. Forbee-X quickly rolled forward to help him lower the sheet to the snow-topped ground. Artoo used the drill feature of the servodriver to poke a hole at the top of the sheet, which was still in the shape of the hull.

"I see," Forbee-X said approvingly. "Very good, Artoo."

"Very good *what*?" Stuart asked. "I don't get it. What's Artoo up to?"

"Well, it's fairly obvious," Threepio said airily.

"Then fill me in," Stuart said.

Threepio didn't have a chance to answer, which was lucky, because he had no idea what Artoo and Forbee-X were doing. Forbee-X plucked a supply pack out of Stuart's hands and placed it on the sheet of metal.

"You see?" Her screen flashed a quick rainbow of colors, something she did when she was excited. Artoo threaded a piece of carbon-spun rope into the hole he had made. "It's a sled. This way we only have to drag the supply packs, not carry them."

Stuart circled the sled as Forbee-X piled on the rest of the supply packs. "It still looks heavy," he observed doubtfully.

Forbee-X's screen flashed the micrograms of the sled's weight. "Even at this weight, a small droid like Artoo should have no trouble pulling the sled," she said. "The friction between the sled and the snow —"

"Friction!" Threepio interrupted excitedly. "I remember that concept! But when we were heading into the planet's atmosphere, you told us that friction slowed things down."

"Right," Stuart agreed. "You said that the pod rubbed against the air to produce friction, which slowed the speed of our descent. So if Artoo's sled rubs against the snow, won't that slow it down, too?"

"That is true," Forbee-X said. Her screen flashed, and a diagram appeared. "Look!"

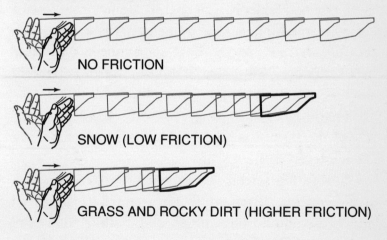

Here's what would happen if you pushed a sled with the same amount of force but different amounts of friction.

NO FRICTION

SNOW (LOW FRICTION)

GRASS AND ROCKY DIRT (HIGHER FRICTION)

"There *is* friction between the sled and the snow," Forbee-X explained. "But if you look at the diagram, you can see that it's quite low. That amount won't slow down the sled."

Artoo beeped and whistled. Threepio was just about to translate when Forbee-X spoke up.

"Yes, Artoo, we're ready," Forbee said.

"I was just about to say that!" Threepio cried.

"Wait, you guys!" Stuart called. "Look at this!"

Stuart pointed to an animal that seemed to be frozen on one of the pod wings. It looked like a lizard, except that it had wings that folded back against its body. Its skin was iridescent, shining colors of green, yellow, and purple. Stuart picked it up gently.

"I can feel its heartbeat," he said. "But it's so cold and still."

"That's because it's a cold-blooded creature," Forbee-X said.

"Cold-blooded?" Stuart asked. "I'm surprised its blood isn't frozen solid." He held it against his body, trying to warm it back up.

Forbee-X's screen shimmered uncertainly, then resolved into its usual cool blue. "Maybe I shouldn't have used the term *cold-blooded*," she told Stuart. "It's more correct to say that the creature is an ectotherm. You, on the other hand, are an endotherm — sometimes called a warm-blooded animal. Look."

Your body stays warm using the energy from your food. That can keep your body temperature high, even in cold weather. In warm weather, you just use less food. And in hot weather, your body has ways of cooling itself off. As a result, your body temperature stays pretty constant.

Endotherm
("warm-blooded")

An ectotherm's temperature changes with the weather, even when it's in perfect health. That's because it can't heat itself with food energy as well as you can. Ectotherms try to stay in a comfortable range. If the weather is too hot, they may hide in the cool shade of a rock. If the weather is too cold, they may crawl on top of the rock to bask in the sun's warming rays.

Ectotherm
("cold-blooded")

"But it doesn't seem to be working," Stuart said worriedly. He stroked the skin of the lizard. "The lizard feels so cold!"

"The temperature is too low for it to survive, I'm afraid," Forbee-X said. "That's why it's so strange to find it here. Maybe it got snared in the pod wing as we flew over a warmer climate. My guess is that if it doesn't return to its home climate, it will die."

Stuart reached into the medpack and withdrew a piece of bandage. He made a sling around his neck and slipped the lizard inside, next to his chest.

"Are you sure you want to do that, Stuart?" Forbee-X asked. "The lizard isn't very large, but we're going a long way. Carrying him could tire you out sooner."

"I'm not leaving him," Stuart said firmly. "Hopefully it will get warmer as the day goes on. Right, Forbee?"

Forbee-X's screen flashed a wintry gray as the snowfall suddenly thickened. "I certainly hope so," she murmured.

But it didn't seem to get warmer. Artoo rolled ahead of them, dragging the sled full of supplies. The snow became a dense white curtain, and they soon lost sight of him.

"Artoo!" Threepio called. His words were snatched by the wind and tossed back at him.

"Don't worry, Threepio," Forbee-X called cheerfully. "Artoo won't get lost. He has the electrocompass."

Time passed in a blur of snow and wind. A weak sun struggled out from behind a cloud and beamed its feeble rays down on them. Stuart stumbled, exhausted from pushing through the wet snow.

"I think we need to rest!" Threepio called to Forbee.

Forbee-X stopped. She contracted her legs and settled into her sitting mode. Her egg-shaped head rotated. "I've been taking temperature readings. It's warming up. And the snow is starting to lift."

"That's good news," Threepio said, peering ahead

for Artoo. He saw his compact friend still moving at the same steady pace. "Oh, there's Artoo, thank goodness," Threepio continued, relieved. "We should tell him we're stopping. Artoo! Artoo!" he shouted.

But just then, as Threepio watched in horror, Artoo fell through the ground and disappeared!

THE BIG THAW

"Where did he go?" Stuart shouted.

"I don't know! I don't know!" Threepio repeated, waving his arms.

Forbee-X extended her legs again and began to move in Artoo's direction. Threepio ran next to her. Suddenly, Forbee-X's arm shot out to slow him down.

"The temperature has warmed and then chilled, making this surface very dangerous," Forbee-X said, walking across the snow at a fast clip, but testing every step. "Can you feel that icy skin on top of the snow, Threepio?"

"Yes, it's very slippery," Threepio said, his arms windmilling furiously as he fought to keep his balance.

"My hypothesis is that when the temperature

rose, the top layer of snow began to melt," Forbee-X explained. "When the temperature dropped, the melted snow froze again. When it refroze, it became a hard crust of ice on top of the other snow. Unfortunately, the crust was not hard enough to withstand the weight of the sled. So Artoo crashed through and fell in a drift. We could not have foreseen this. It happened with surprising speed! On Delantine, a crust like this would normally form after a sunny spring day followed by a freezing cold night. Don't worry. We'll get him out!"

As they drew closer to where Artoo had disappeared, Forbee-X called his name. "Artoo? Where are you?"

They heard a faint beep.

"He's all right! Thank heavens," Threepio said.

"Don't move," Forbee-X warned. "Stuart, you're the lightest. We're going to tie a rope around your waist. We don't want to lose you, too. Lie flat and squiggle yourself over the ice until you can see Artoo."

"All right," Stuart agreed. He untied the sling and handed the lizard to Threepio. "Will you hold the lizard?"

"Anything," Threepio said. "Just hurry!"

Forbee-X lifted one leg, then the other. Spikes shot out from the bottom of her feet. She planted herself in the snow. She took hold of the rope that Stuart had tied around his waist. It would serve as a safety line. Then she handed Stuart another rope and kept the other end. That rope would be used to haul Artoo and the supplies out of the crevasse.

Inch by inch, Stuart slithered over the ice-encrusted snow. Any moment he expected to crash through the ice. He could feel it shifting beneath him. But at last he reached the lip of the crevasse. Cautiously, he eased his head over the side.

"Get you out in a second, Artoo!" he called. He tossed the rope down to Artoo and watched while the droid tied it to the sled and made sure the supplies were lashed securely. Then Stuart gave the thumbs-up sign to Forbee.

Forbee-X pulled up the sled, hand-over-hand. As soon as it hit the lip of the hole, Stuart hauled it over the edge and pushed it back on the ice toward Forbee-X and Threepio.

"Now for Artoo," Threepio said.

Artoo clasped the rope with his pincer claw. Forbee-X settled herself into the ground and pulled, using all her strength. Artoo slammed against the side of the crevasse. Snow cascaded down on his head. Artoo beeped indignantly.

"Careful, Forbee!" Stuart called. "We don't want to bury him! Go slower."

With beeps and whirrs and one long whistle, Artoo finally appeared over the edge of the hole. Stuart reached out and grabbed him. Together with Forbee-X, he pulled him over the edge. With a shrill whistle, Artoo landed on his side.

"Hang on, Artoo," Stuart said, grinning. He righted the droid, and Artoo rolled to safety, beeping furiously.

"It's all right, Artoo," Threepio said, hurrying toward him. "It's just your dignity that's hurt."

Forbee-X's antennae rose. "It's getting warm. And look at the trees! How curious. It's like instant spring!"

Only minutes before, they had been trudging through a heavy snowstorm. But now, green buds were appearing on the trees. The snow was melting beneath their feet and turning to mud. Threepio saw wildflowers in the meadow ahead, as though they'd sprung up in mere minutes.

Stuart turned toward Threepio. "I'll take the lizard back," he said.

Threepio eased the sling from around his neck and handed it to Stuart.

"Let's continue," Forbee-X said. Her egg-shaped head rotated, her circuits clicking. The warmth of the sun would soon dry the mud, and the temperature was rising a few degrees a minute. It was perfect traveling weather, with a clear blue sky and not a cloud in sight.

But a moment later, a shadow fell over the sun.

"Well, that's curious," Forbee-X murmured.

They all looked up. The dark cloud separated into individual shapes. Wings flapped in unison, accompanied by a distant *caw caw.*

"Birds," Stuart said. He took out the macrobinoculars to study them.

"What huge creatures," Forbee-X observed. "They're almost as big as bonegnawers."

Threepio shuddered. "Oh, please don't mention those terrible creatures. Their huge, teeth-filled jaws can crush *boulders,* let alone a droid. If those creatures are anything like bonegnawers, I say we lay low."

Artoo beeped a "yes," and Forbee-X nodded.

"No sense in attracting attention," she agreed. "Do you see those rocks ahead? They could provide cover. I suggest we —"

But Forbee-X didn't get to finish her thought. Suddenly, the lizard that had been dormant in the sling poked its head out of Stuart's jacket. It emitted a series of earsplitting shrieks.

"Will you get that thing to quiet down?" Threepio hissed.

"Shhhh," Stuart said, trying to hold the squirming lizard against his body. The lizard jerked its head and began to shriek again. The sound bounced off the rocks and echoed in the stillness.

"Oh, dear," Forbee-X said. "I'm afraid the birds heard the lizard!"

Artoo beeped frantically. Threepio watched in horror as the birds wheeled in formation and turned.

The birds were heading straight for them!

CLAWS

Without a word, Stuart and the droids took off for the shelter of the boulders. Shadows fell over them as the birds flew lower, their giant wings beating rhythmically. The group scrambled over the rocks, looking for a crevice big enough to hide in. "Here!" Stuart called. He slithered into the crack.

Forbee-X's arms shot out and extended even longer. She grasped Artoo in her strong fingers and deposited him in the crevice.

"Now you, Threepio!" she cried.

Threepio didn't need any more encouragement. He hoisted himself down into the crack.

The bird flying at the top of the V formation suddenly swooped down, its claws extended.

"Forbee!" Threepio screamed.

Forbee-X's legs extended, shooting her down into the hole. The frustrated bird wheeled, cawing angrily.

"That was close," Threepio breathed.

"It's not over yet," Forbee-X said worriedly. "Those beaks look awfully long. We need something to block that hole!"

Threepio screamed as the bird shoved its beak into the hole, missing him by millimeters. Forbee-X's hand shot out and she slammed the beak hard. With a *caw*, the bird retreated.

"Stuart, Artoo, Threepio, look for smaller rocks," Forbee-X directed. "Quickly!"

Threepio reached down for the biggest stone he could find. He handed it to Forbee-X. Stuart found a long, flat rock, which he handed to her. Forbee-X wedged the rocks into the opening, leaving just a tiny crack. She only hoped it would hold.

More birds arrived, cawing furiously. The lizard suddenly began to screech again.

"Stuart, hold the lizard's mouth shut!" Threepio screamed.

"I can't!" Stuart panted. "He keeps twisting away."

The screeching bounced off the rocks and echoed, driving the birds into a frenzy. Threepio shrank back as he heard the scratch of their claws against the stones. The birds shrieked with fury as they tried to force their way into the opening. One bird shoved its slender beak into the crack between the stones. Forbee-X rapped the beak with a sharp stone. With an earsplitting cry, the bird angrily retreated.

But soon, the birds grew tired of their effort. One bird took off, wheeling in a circle around the others. After a few halfhearted pecks, the other birds followed.

"Whew," Stuart said. "I thought we were bird food, for sure." He peeked into the sling and petted the lizard gently. "Are you okay, little fellow?"

"Him? What about *us*?" Threepio shuddered.

Forbee-X yanked at the flat stone, trying to dislodge it. "I think I wedged this in a little too tightly."

"Oh, dear," Threepio moaned. "Now we're buried alive! What could possibly happen next?"

"Maybe Artoo can help with a pincer claw." Stuart suggested.

Artoo tried to jimmy the rock free with the thin edge of a driver. With a burst of effort, the rock flew out of the opening, almost hitting Threepio in the head.

"Artoo, really!" he exclaimed. "Maybe Forbee should give you another lesson in how friction works."

Shakily, the group climbed out of the crevice. They scanned the sky above, which was empty. Artoo picked up the sled rope, and they continued on their journey.

The weather continued to warm as they walked. Forbee-X's antennae kept rising and trembling as she took reading after reading.

"I just don't understand this," she murmured worriedly. "And I don't like it, either."

"What's there to worry about?" Stuart asked cheerfully. "Traveling over grass is much easier than traveling over snow. We're making good time."

Artoo whistled a protest. He was having trouble dragging the sled.

"Let me help you, Artoo," Stuart offered. He took hold of the rope and walked alongside Artoo. After a few minutes, he stopped and wiped his forehead. "Whew. This *is* hard work. Artoo made it look easy earlier."

"That's because he pulled the sled over snow, not grass," Forbee-X said. "Remember when I described higher friction? It's slowing the sled down more, making it harder to pull. You can always count on science to follow the rules!"

"That's a great explanation, Forbee," Stuart said grumpily. "But it doesn't make it any easier to pull the sled. Why don't we just leave it here? We could load the supplies into packs."

"Good idea, Stuart," Threepio agreed.

Artoo flashed his lights and beeped.

"Artoo has a point," Forbee-X said. "The sled could come in handy later."

"Well, of course you'll side with *him*," Threepio grumbled.

Artoo chirped, then ended on a whistle that sounded awfully sarcastic to Threepio. Then he snatched up the rope to the sled and trundled away, dragging the sled behind him.

"Oh, dear," Threepio fretted. "Now he's gone off in a huff. Artoo can be so sensitive!"

Stuart ran ahead as Artoo disappeared around a bend. A moment later, they heard a *whoop*.

"He did it! Artoo did it!" Stuart yelled.

"Did *what*?" Threepio muttered as Forbee-X zoomed ahead. "Why am I always the last to know?"

Threepio rounded the bend. Ahead, he saw Stuart, Forbee-X, and Artoo standing by a rushing blue river. Now Threepio could hear the sound of the water coursing over rocks and pebbles.

"Artoo heard the river!" Stuart shouted.

"But my auditory sensors are just as refined as his," Threepio complained as he picked his way over the rocks at the river's edge. "I didn't hear a thing."

"Maybe because you were jabbering so much, Threepio," Stuart teased.

Artoo busily unloaded supplies from the sled. He placed them on the rocks nearby.

"So you've decided to leave the sled after all?" Threepio asked. "I'm glad you see it my way, Artoo. I always say —"

Artoo dragged the sled over to the river. He pushed it in, keeping careful hold on the rope. It bobbed in the shallow water.

"Excellent!" Forbee-X's screen flashed a rainbow.

"It's a boat!" Stuart cried. "What a hypergalactic idea, Artoo. Now we can really move!"

Threepio regarded the sled dubiously. "But will it hold all of us? May I point out that I am made of metal? *I* certainly don't float."

Forbee-X's screen flashed a cheerful blue. "Density is the key to floating. It describes something's weight compared to its size. Watch."

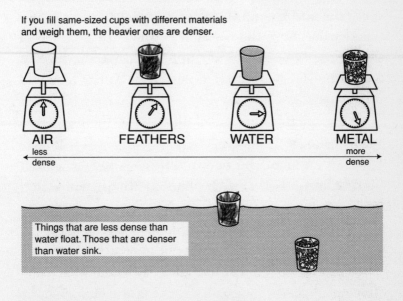

If you fill same-sized cups with different materials and weigh them, the heavier ones are denser.

AIR — less dense   FEATHERS   WATER   METAL — more dense

Things that are less dense than water float. Those that are denser than water sink.

"But the sled, I mean the boat, is metal," Stuart said. "Metal is denser than water. So how could we possibly float?"

"Look inside the boat," Forbee-X prompted. "What is it filled with?"

Together, Threepio and Stuart peered into the boat. "All I see are the supplies and some scrap metal Artoo salvaged from the pod," Threepio said.

"What else do you see?" Forbee-X directed.

"Nothing," Stuart said. "Just air." Then his face brightened. "Oh, I get it! Air is less dense than water. But why wouldn't the boat just sink while the air floated?"

Forbee-X's screen beamed yellow. "In this case, the air inside the boat's sides counts as part of the boat. Let's use an example. Say you could take the boat, the scraps, and the air, and put them in a turbo-blender. Suppose the result was a perfect mixture of the three. If you took a cupful of that mixture, it would be less dense than a cupful of water. It would float."

"But what if you added all of us to the blender?" Stuart asked.

"A cupful of the new mixture would be denser than before," Forbee-X explained. "But it would still be less dense than water. So —"

"We would float!" Stuart concluded.

"I'm not sure I like being put in a turbo-blender," Threepio noted. "But I *am* glad to hear that I won't sink."

"So let's get going!" Stuart said excitedly. He

turned to Forbee-X and Artoo. "Sorry I ever doubted you guys. You were totally right about finding the river. I won't argue with the two brains again!"

"Excuse me, Master Stuart," Threepio said. "Aren't you forgetting something?" He waited for Stuart to mention that Threepio had a helpful brain, too.

"Oh, right!" Stuart said. "I left the macrobinoculars on that rock!"

Threepio lowered himself into the boat in a huff. Nobody noticed his mood, which just proved how neglected he was. Artoo and Stuart followed. Forbee-X stood by, her screen slowly flashing from color to color. It meant she was pondering a problem.

Artoo beeped a question at her.

"No, I'm all right, Artoo," Forbee-X said. "There's something nagging at me, but I can't quite place it."

"Sorry, Forbee, but we don't have time for you to figure it out," Stuart said impatiently. "We're burning daylight here."

"Daylight can't *burn*, Stuart," Forbee-X explained. "Actually, it —"

"He means that we're wasting time," Threepio interrupted, afraid Forbee-X would launch into another lecture.

"That's right," Stuart said anxiously. "Now we only have thirty-five hours to make contact!"

Forbee-X stepped into the boat. "You see, the

thing is —" she began, but her words ended in a very unscientific *whoop* as Stuart threw off the rope and the boat whirled away down the river.

"Weeee-oooooo!" Stuart yodeled.

"This is certainly an improvement on walking," Threepio said, settling himself on one side of the boat.

At first, the boat sailed along smoothly. Then the craft picked up speed, causing Threepio to grip the side nervously. Spray hit their faces as the boat bounced along with the fast current.

"We're speeding up!" Stuart called. The wind blew his dark hair away from his intent face. "This is great! We'll make good time."

"Oh, dear," Forbee-X said.

"What?" Stuart asked.

"High water," Forbee-X said. "It's logical that the river would run high, considering how quickly everything thawed. I wish we'd stopped to make paddles."

"But the current is carrying us so fast," Threepio said. "Why would we need to paddle? It's just wasted effort."

"The paddles would help us steer," Forbee-X explained.

"Steer around what?" Stuart asked. The boat got caught in an eddy, then popped free and whirled onward, faster than before.

"Rocks, for one thing," Forbee-X said. "Because

if we meet one at high speed, we could be in trouble. And what if we need to get to shore?"

"You worry too much, Forbee," Stuart said. "And —" Suddenly, he stopped. "What's that noise? Is it voices? It's like a murmur."

"That's not conversation you're hearing, Stuart," Forbee-X said worriedly. "That's what I've been trying to tell you. It's rapids!"

WHITE WATER

The boat shot forward around a bend. Ahead they could see foaming white water. Rocks and boulders rose out of the churning water.

"Any scientific suggestions, Forbee?" Stuart yelled over the sound of the rapids.

"Yes," Forbee-X answered. Her arms shot out and her fingers grasped each side of the boat. "Hang on!"

Suddenly, the bow plunged into the churning water. Artoo went flying, and Threepio grabbed him just in time. But it was hard to keep hold of Artoo and the boat at the same time. As the boat hit another rapid and flew into the air, Threepio shrieked. He'd lost his grip on the boat *and* Artoo! He saved himself from falling into the river just in time.

Forbee-X extended her legs and grabbed Artoo. She was able to intertwine her long steel toes to keep him secure.

The force of the water suddenly sent the boat skimming sideways, straight into a boulder. Threepio screamed as they smashed against it.

"We're doomed!" Threepio cried.

With an awful scraping noise, the boat popped free and whirled on. Caught in an eddy, the boat swirled for an instant, then shot forward over a small waterfall. Threepio gasped as they hung in midair for a moment, then crashed down into the turbulent river. A wave of water hit them, almost swamping the boat.

"We're going to drown!" Threepio yelled.

Forbee extended her arms. Metal expanded into webs between each finger, creating makeshift paddles. She dipped her hands into the water, trying to steer the boat away from the biggest boulders as it pitched and bucked.

Through the mist ahead they could see another patch of turbulent water. Now Threepio was aware of a roaring noise.

"Waterfall!" Threepio cried, terrified.

"We have to get ashore!" Forbee-X yelled.

She dug into the surging water. The boat careened through the rapids, slamming against the water again and again. But Forbee-X managed to reach calmer water at the edge of the river. Stuart jumped out to pull them to shore.

They stepped out of the boat, relieved to be on land again.

"You really saved the day, Forbee," Stuart said admiringly. He checked the lizard inside the sling — it looked okay, but nervous.

"What about me?" Threepio spoke up. "I helped, too."

"You mean by screaming 'we're doomed' every two seconds?" Stuart asked with a grin.

Artoo gave a long whistle.

"It isn't funny, Artoo," Threepio grumbled.

"I think you can all see that paddles are necessary if we want to complete our journey on the river," Forbee-X pointed out.

Stuart scanned the ground around them. He picked up a fallen limb. "How about this, Forbee? Will this work?"

Forbee-X gripped the end of the limb and hefted it. "This will make an excellent shaft," she told Stuart. "We'll need something wider as a paddle blade."

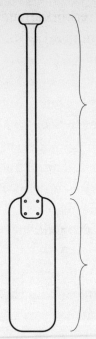

Shaft–Should be straight and thin enough to grip easily.

Blade–This is the part that goes in the water. It should be flat and wide.

Artoo trundled off toward the makeshift boat. He reached in and brought out a thin sheet of scrap metal from one of the packs. It was oval-shaped, flat, and smooth. He showed it to Forbee-X.

"Perfect, Artoo," Forbee-X approved. "We can use the macrofuser to shape it."

Threepio felt left out again. He wasn't terribly good at making things. He could make a good *impression,* of course. But paddles were another thing altogether.

He watched as Artoo macrofused the metal until

it was a smooth, perfect oval. Stuart whittled the limbs into shafts. Then they fastened the metal blade to the shaft by using a small beamdrill and carbon screws.

Stuart held up the finished paddles. "Forbee, how do you use these things, anyway? I've never been in a boat without hydrosteering."

"It's very simple," Forbee-X replied. "The Third Law of Motion says that for every push, there is an equal and opposite push. So you'll push on the water . . ."

"And the water will push back on the paddle?" Stuart asked doubtfully.

"Let's get back in the river, and I'll show you," Forbee-X suggested. "But first, we need to bypass the waterfall."

Threepio and Stuart carried the boat, and Forbee-X and Artoo carried the rest of the supplies. They slithered downhill past the roaring waterfall until they reached calmer water. Then they relaunched the boat.

Stuart and Threepio sat in the middle of the boat on opposite sides. Forbee-X handed each of them a paddle. Then she pushed the boat gently off the bank and stepped in.

Threepio dipped his paddle and pushed hard against the water while Stuart did the same. The boat swung in a circle.

"No, Threepio!" Forbee-X cried, clutching the

sides of the boat. "You have to dip your paddle forward, then back! Not back, then forward. We'll go in
a circle forever."

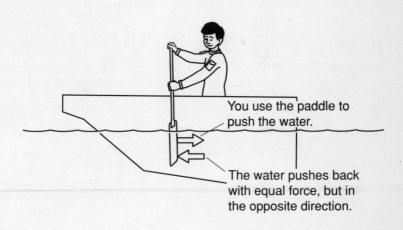

You use the paddle to push the water.

The water pushes back with equal force, but in the opposite direction.

"But equal force sounds like a tug-of-war," Stuart
protested as he studied the diagram. "It seems like
neither the boat nor the water would move. Why does
the boat move forward?"

Forbee-X's screen cleared. "It is very much like a
tug-of-war, only with pushes instead of pulls. Watch."

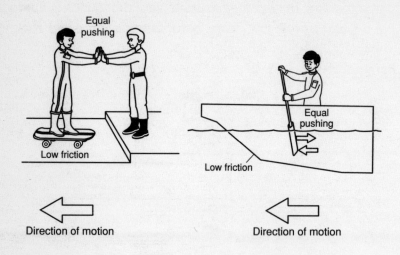

Equal pushing

Low friction

Direction of motion

Equal pushing

Low friction

Direction of motion

"That's easy," Stuart said. "The other guy would win, no contest. There's no way I could stand my ground with wheels under my feet."

"Why not?" Forbee-X prompted.

Stuart frowned, thinking. "My opponent could keep a grip on the ground because of the friction between it and his feet," he said. "Wheels reduce friction, right? So I'd get shoved away because of lower friction."

"You are a born scientist, Stuart!" Forbee-X said,

her screen glowing. "Compare that to the 'pushing contest' between you and the river water. Several forces help the water 'stand its ground.' Meanwhile, the friction between your boat and the water is low. As a result, you and your boat are easily pushed forward. Like this."

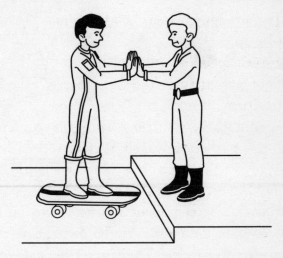

What if you were in a pushing contest with an equally strong opponent? Your opponent stands on solid ground, but you are on a skatecoaster. Who would win?

Threepio and Stuart began paddling again. It took a few minutes to get themselves in synch. But soon they were moving swiftly down the river.

Suddenly, Stuart burst out laughing.

"What's so funny?" Threepio asked. "I'm trying as hard as I can."

"It's the lizard," Stuart explained. "He's tickling me." Carefully, he withdrew the squirming lizard from the sling around his neck.

The lizard turned its head to check out its surroundings. It blinked in a lazy sort of way, then crawled up Stuart's arm and sat on his shoulder.

"Hey, little guy," Stuart said, smiling. "Looks like you woke up."

Artoo chirped and whirred.

"What was that, Artoo?" Forbee-X asked. "It's going to storm?"

"He said it's very *warm*," Threepio corrected triumphantly. Forbee-X wasn't perfect! "And look — there's fruit on that tree now. When we landed, there were only leaves."

Forbee-X's screen went murky. "I've been trying to compute data since we landed. These climate changes are too sudden. They aren't logical, yet they exist — a true puzzle for a scientist. But I think I've developed a theory about Planet X. I know it sounds incredible, but I believe this place experiences four seasons in one day. This morning, it was snowing. The trees were bare. Then, only hours later, the snow melted."

"And Artoo crashed through a drift," Threepio remembered. "Poor Artoo!"

"Then the trees grew leaves," Forbee-X went on. "Flowers bloomed. Evidence of spring, correct? And now, look around. The leaves are full and green. The fruit is ripe, and the grass is long. Summer."

"But how could the seasons go by so fast?" Stuart asked. "They last for months back home."

"I don't know yet," Forbee-X said. "But when you try to solve a puzzle, you start with what you know. Let's look at how the seasons work on a planet like Delantine."

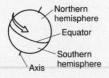

Northern hemisphere
Equator
Southern hemisphere
Axis

Delantine has a tilted axis. (An axis, as you may remember from our spinning escape pod, is an imaginary line that something spins around.) Because of this tilt, when it is summer in the northern hemisphere, it is winter in the southern hemisphere.

Summer: As you can see, the northern hemisphere is receiving more sunlight, and the most intense sunlight. Lots of intense sunlight makes for warmer temperatures—summer.

Winter: Meanwhile, the southern hemisphere receives less sunlight. That lack of sunlight makes for colder temperatures—winter.

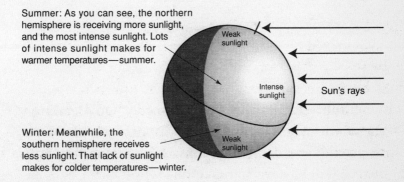

Weak sunlight

Intense sunlight

Sun's rays

Weak sunlight

"Okay, that explains how we get one season, but how do we get the others?" Stuart asked.

"How about another diagram?" Forbee-X asked.

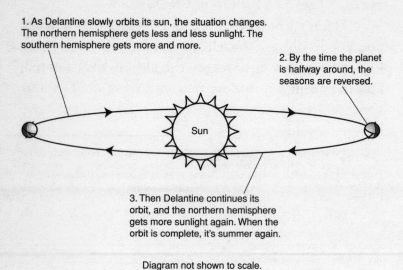

1. As Delantine slowly orbits its sun, the situation changes. The northern hemisphere gets less and less sunlight. The southern hemisphere gets more and more.

2. By the time the planet is halfway around, the seasons are reversed.

Sun

3. Then Delantine continues its orbit, and the northern hemisphere gets more sunlight again. When the orbit is complete, it's summer again.

Diagram not shown to scale.

"You see?" Forbee-X continued. "On Delantine, the whole orbit takes a year — just over 365 days. But to get the speeded-up seasons we're seeing here, this planet would have to make one whole orbit between sunrise and sunset. It would then make another whole orbit overnight."

"That sounds impossible," Stuart objected.

"My calculations agree with you," Forbee-X said. "But you can't argue with reality, Stuart. Observation is the scientist's best friend."

"This is some hyper-wacky planet," Stuart said as he tucked the lizard back in the sling.

"Yes, it is," Threepio agreed. "I can't wait to leave it."

The sun traveled across the sky as they floated, keeping them warm despite a gathering chill. Stuart kept watch anxiously, sure that around the next bend the city would appear.

Artoo gave a series of chirps and whirrs, and Forbee-X and Threepio both glanced at the riverbank.

"What did he say?" Stuart asked, stroking with his paddle.

"It's fall," Threepio said. "Look, the leaves have changed color."

"Animals adapt to seasonal changes, too," Forbee-X said. "Some animals grow a heavier fur coat to keep themselves warm in winter. Other animals hibernate, sleeping through winter. Birds sometimes migrate — they fly to warmer places during the cold winter months. Often, they travel in groups called —"

"Flocks!" Stuart guessed. "The birds that attacked us came from the south. Maybe they were migrating north for the summer."

"Excellent deduction, Stuart," Forbee-X approved.

"So they don't live around here?" Threepio asked. "That's reassuring, I must say."

"Wait a second," Stuart said. "If they migrated north in spring, wouldn't they migrate back south again?"

"Very good, Stuart," Forbee-X said. "I would say that is exactly what they would do."

"So, wouldn't they migrate in the fall?" Stuart continued.

"Ah," Forbee-X said. "An excellent, if somewhat disturbing, deduction."

"Oh, dear," Threepio said. "I think I see what you're getting at."

They drifted with the current for a moment. All was eerily quiet. Everyone scanned the sky nervously.

Then Threepio heard it. A distant *caw caw* that sounded terribly familiar.

"Stuart, don't let that —" Threepio began frantically. But it was too late. The lizard suddenly popped its head out of Stuart's sling and began to screech again!

"Throw that creature overboard!" Threepio yelled over the sound of the lizard.

But it was too late.

The great wings of the birds beat steadily, carrying them swiftly toward the group. The sky grew black with their numbers. And this time, there was nowhere to hide.

AIRBORNE

Threepio frantically dug his paddle into the river. Stuart still had his paddle raised above the water as he struggled to keep the lizard in the sling. The boat swung wildly to the left, toward the middle of the river.

"Stop, Threepio!" Forbee-X shouted. The boat began to turn in a circle. "We're going nowhere!"

Artoo chirped insistently.

"He said it's too late —" Forbee-X began.

"— so we should —" Threepio continued.

"— protect Stuart —" Forbee-X interrupted.

"— by covering him with our bodies!" Threepio got out in a frantic rush.

They could hear the rush of wind as the great wings of the birds beat steadily, coming nearer. Stuart threw himself on the bottom of the boat. Artoo's arms

44

shot out, and he suspended himself over Stuart's head. Threepio arranged himself over Stuart, trying to protect as much of the boy's body as he could. Finally, Forbee-X's arms and feet elongated and planted on the bottom of the boat, suspending her over them all.

"Let them try to attack us now!" Forbee-X said grimly.

Threepio was glad Stuart was protected, but he felt terribly exposed. If he got through this adventure without needing a new casing, he'd be lucky. That is, if the birds' sharp beaks didn't penetrate his circuits and put him out of commission altogether!

The great birds swooped down on them. Threepio felt sharp claws deliver a deep scratch down his flank.

"Oh, dear!" he moaned.

"Oh, deeeeeaarrrr!" Forbee-X suddenly screamed as she rose three feet off the boat. The bird had grabbed her with its claws, and was strong enough to carry her away!

"Nooooooo!" Threepio screamed. He grabbed onto Forbee-X's dangling foot. "Let her go, you overgrown feathered beast!"

"Ohhhhhhh!" Forbee-X yelled as the bird began to rise.

"Heeellllppp!" Threepio screamed as he began to rise with her. The bird was even more powerful than he imagined. But he refused to let go of Forbee-X's foot. He wouldn't let the bird take her away!

Forbee-X managed to work both her arms free. They lengthened until her long fingers could grasp the edges of the boat. Startled, the bird loosened its grip. Forbee crashed down into the boat again, taking Threepio with her.

"Good work, Forbee!" Threepio panted. "That was clos-ohhhhh!"

The boat tilted alarmingly, almost spilling them backward into the river. The bird had gripped the bow of the boat. Threepio saw water inches from his face. Then another huge bird swooped down and stretched its claws around the stern. The two birds then carried the boat between them, up into the air. Forbee-X gripped the sides of the boat, stabilizing the craft.

"Whoooaaaa!" Threepio screamed as they rose, higher and higher.

"What's happening? What's happening?" Stuart shouted. From his position on the bottom of the boat, he couldn't see a thing.

"We appear to be flying," Forbee-X answered. "I think you can all sit up now. We're fine."

"Considering we're in a tiny scrap of metal being carried by two ravenous flying beasts," Threepio said nervously.

Stuart peered over the side of the boat. "I just hope they don't drop us. We've left the river. It would be a hard landing."

"Please don't even mention the possibility," Threepio said.

"Don't worry," Forbee-X said. "These birds are excellent flying machines."

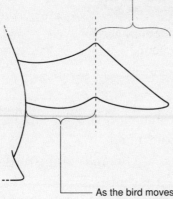

Like many flying creatures, this bird has wings that are divided into two sections. Each section has a job. The flapping of the outer wing propels the bird forward. In fact, it works something like a boat paddle, only it pushes against air instead of water.

As the bird moves forward, the inner wing provides lift—or upward force. That is what is keeping us in the air.

"You may remember lift as the force that kept our escape pod in the air as Stuart piloted us in for our emergency landing," Forbee-X explained. "Each bird's inner wing has a shape similar to that of the pod's wings."

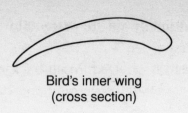

Bird's inner wing
(cross section)

Escape pod's emergency wing
(cross section)

"You see, it's this basic shape, called an airfoil, that creates lift," Forbee-X continued.

"That's marvelous news," Threepio approved. "As long as it keeps us in the air, that is."

Artoo beeped and whirred.

"Good question, Artoo," Forbee-X said. "And we're in luck. The direction we're traveling in is south. Exactly where we want to go!"

"And we'll get there faster this way," Stuart said, peering over the side again. The boat rocked a bit when he shifted his weight.

"Please don't do that, Master Stuart!" Threepio

begged. "I was finally able to pretend I was riding in a nice, stable airspeeder."

Stuart carefully settled himself back in the bottom of the craft. "Why do you think the birds took us, Forbee?"

"Do we really need to know?" Threepio asked comfortably. "This is so much more pleasant than hiking. Let's watch this glorious sunset."

"I'm afraid we should be prepared for the answer to Stuart's question," Forbee-X said thoughtfully. "I can think of two reasons why the birds took us. One, for nest building."

"Nest building?" Threepio asked doubtfully. "But we're not terribly comfortable. All this metal. Even *I* wouldn't want to nest on me."

"Birds scavenge all kinds of things for nests," Forbee-X explained. "And we don't know the habits of these particular birds. They might make complicated structures. But I think it's more likely that they consider us a possible food source. When we get back to their nests, they'll discover that the droids are quite inedible."

"What will they do with us?" Threepio asked in alarm.

"Discard us, most likely," Forbee-X answered. "From a very significant height, I'm sure. Stuart, on the other hand, will make a tasty treat."

"Uh, thanks, Forbee," Stuart said. He looked green. "All of a sudden, I don't feel so good."

"Don't worry, Stuart," Forbee-X said, beaming a cheerful yellow at him. "We're not licked yet."

Artoo beeped several times.

"That's right, Artoo!" Threepio said. "We forgot about the parachute! Maybe we should fasten it to the boat, just in case the birds get tired of carrying us."

"That's not a bad idea," Forbee-X agreed. "It must be in one of the supply packs."

Stuart reached down to pick up a pack. But before he could open it, they heard a loud angry *caw* above them. A fellow bird, larger and stronger than the birds that carried the boat, suddenly dived at the bird carrying the bow. Its beak tore into the smaller bird's flesh.

"I'm afraid our birds are under attack," Forbee-X said, just as the predator rammed into the smaller bird again, shaking the boat. Forbee-X gripped the boat more tightly, trying to stabilize the craft. Then the bird that was carrying the bow loosened its grip, and the boat tipped to one side.

"Maybe we should do something about that parachute," Forbee-X called nervously.

"Too late!" Threepio screamed as the bird dropped the bow completely. "We're going down!"

FREE FALL

The boat tilted alarmingly, almost spilling them out. But the bird who had been carrying the bow lunged and grabbed it again just in time. The boat stabilized as the carrier birds beat their wings in unison and cawed furiously, protecting their treasure.

But the attacking bird didn't fly away. With a ferocious cry, it dove toward the smaller bird once again. The predator tore at the bird's flesh while the smaller bird tried to defend itself with its sharp beak. The bird's mate at the stern screeched a warning.

"Oh, my!" Forbee-X yelled over the crying of the three birds. "I had no idea these birds would fight over us!"

Threepio felt paralyzed with fear. Every time the boat tipped, he saw blue sky rush up at him. The ground tilted crazily far, far below.

Stuart scrambled frantically through the supply packs. "I can't find the parachute!"

"Attack coming in toward the rear!" Forbee-X's screen flashed crazily. "Hang on!"

This time, the attacking bird chose to assault the bird at the stern. Claws outstretched, beak open, it struck again and again in a frenzied attack. The predator dug its claws into the neck of the smaller bird.

The craft tilted as the smaller bird tried to twist away. Then, shrieking, it began to dive, and the bird carrying the bow followed.

Wind whistled past the craft as it plummeted hundreds of feet in seconds. Stuart yelled and Threepio screamed as the boat tilted crazily.

Then the two carrier birds stabilized, their wings flapping furiously.

"Whew," Stuart said. "That was close."

"As close as I ever want to get to falling," Threepio said. He peeked down at the ground. Through the dusk, he could just make out the terrain. "It looks like sand."

Stuart peeked over, too. "And spiny plants. Ouch!"

"At least we're at a lower altitude," Forbee-X said. "Just in case we're dropped."

"Please don't say that," Threepio moaned. "I'm sure the other bird has given up. But just in case, Stuart, find that parachute!"

"Here it comes again!" Forbee-X shouted.

Claws outstretched, the predator dropped on top of the back of the bird holding the bow. The attacker's claws ripped into the smaller bird's flesh and stayed there. With a shriek of pain, the carrier bird dropped the boat and took off, with the predator still pecking and clawing at its body.

Now the boat hung straight down, suspended from the claws of the bird holding the stern. The droids and Threepio held onto the sides, their feet dangling in midair. Forbee-X managed to catch one of the supply boxes with her toes, but the rest rained down onto the land below.

"Eeeeeeeee!" Threepio screamed.

"Let's just hope the other bird doesn't let goooooooooooo!" Forbee-X screamed as the bird suddenly dropped the boat and flew off.

They only had time to feel sheer terror as the ground rushed up at them. Dots of color turned into plants. Smudges of gray turned into rocks.

Threepio closed his eyes. He pictured his metal body scattered over the landscape. A golden arm here, a shiny foot there.

And then they landed with an *oof* and a *squish*.

A *squish*?

Cautiously, Threepio opened his eyes. They had landed on a huge plant!

"What is this thing?" Stuart asked.

Forbee-X scratched at the plant, her screen flashing with data. "It's a succulent," she said. "It's adapted to dry desert conditions. This thick skin helps the plant store water. That's what saved us."

"Well, I'm very grateful to it," Threepio said fervently. "It saved us from a ghastly end, I'm sure."

Stuart unzipped his survival suit to check on the lizard. It lay against his body, its eyes closed as though it were asleep.

"It's getting dark," Forbee-X said worriedly. "I suggest we locate as many supplies as we can."

The boat and many of the boxes had also landed on or near the plant. Stuart and the droids canvassed the area and found most of the supplies. They gathered them and stacked them by the boat, then wearily climbed into it for shelter.

Stuart shivered. "It's awfully cold. I thought deserts were hot, Forbee."

"Look up at the sky," Forbee-X instructed.

The first stars of evening were beginning to twinkle. They looked bright against the deepening blue of the sky.

"No clouds," Forbee-X said. "Deserts have very little cloud cover. That's what causes them to change temperature rapidly. They can reach temperatures of well over a hundred degrees during the day, then lose up to eighty of those degrees at night."

"That's exactly what Tatooine is like," Threepio said. "What a ghastly planet. It's either too hot or too cold."

Artoo beeped his agreement.

"The worst is that there is no shade, either," Threepio complained. "You could fry a kroyie egg on my shell."

"In the desert, not only is there little shade from plant life, there is little shade from clouds," Forbee-X agreed. "Most of the sun's rays reach the ground, making temperatures soar higher. Then, at night, there are no clouds to act as insulation."

"Insulation?" Stuart asked. "Could you explain that, Forbee?"

"Do you think she'd actually say no?" Threepio murmured. Artoo beeped at him, warning him to be nice.

"I'd be delighted, Stuart." Forbee-X beamed a cheerful yellow screen. "Simply put, insulation is something that keeps heat in — or out. If you lie in bed in a cold room, the heat travels from your body into the cold air around you. You get chilly. A blanket would act as insulation, keeping more heat in your body."

"Blanket!" Threepio exclaimed. "Artoo, we must find that parachute for Stuart."

Artoo and Threepio began to dig through the supply boxes.

"On the other hand," Forbee-X continued, "if you carry a cold drink outside on a hot day, heat travels from the hot air into the cold liquid. Soon, your drink is warm. A thermos would act as insulation, keeping the heat out of your cold drink."

"Can we go back to the part about keeping heat *in*?" Stuart asked, shivering.

"Certainly," Forbee-X answered brightly. "At night, a layer of clouds acts much like a blanket. It keeps more heat in the air near the ground. But in a desert, the heat easily travels upward, away from the ground."

"Here it is!" Threepio cried, flourishing the spun-carbon parachute. "It may not have saved us from that nasty fall, but it might keep you warm, Stuart." He drew the parachute around Stuart, but the boy continued to shiver.

Artoo reached down into the bottom of the boat and brought up the scrap metal he'd stored. Then he beeped and whistled at Threepio, who handed him the tools.

"I don't know what you're going to do with those," Threepio stated. "You can't make another blanket out of scrap metal."

"I'm worried about the lizard," Stuart said. "I don't know if he can survive the cold."

"I'm more worried about you, Master Stuart," Threepio fussed.

Stuart shivered. "I can stand it for a few hours. Isn't spring a few hours away, Forbee?"

"Not during the night, I'm afraid," Forbee-X told him. "The seasons are caused by sunlight. We only see the changes during the day. The nights would still be very cold. You'll have to wait until morning until you're warm again."

Stuart groaned.

"The temperatures will be very hot for travel tomorrow," Forbee-X continued. "We'll have to rest often."

"But we'll lose so much time!" Stuart protested. "If we don't find the Rebels, they'll leave without us! Then we'll be stranded here. And I'll lose my chance to rescue Father," he finished brokenly.

"I'm sorry, Stuart. You'll lose strength if we don't take frequent breaks," Forbee-X reminded him softly. "You're not used to a desert climate. We'll go as fast as we can, but the sand will slow us down."

"The sand!" Threepio moaned. "Oh, my poor joints!"

Stuart set his jaw. "There must be a faster way to get out of here."

They heard a hiss, and then a bright flame of light shot up from the bottom of the boat.

"Artoo made a stove out of scrap metal and the rest of the fuel!" Threepio told Stuart excitedly. "Here, Master Stuart. Move closer."

Stuart held his hands out to the heat source. "That feels good. Thanks, Artoo."

"I suggest we turn in," Forbee-X said gently. "It's been a very long day."

They settled down for the night. The light of the stove and Forbee-X's radiant red screen made a comforting glow against the darkness. Stuart slept, and the droids took turns shutting down their circuits so that someone would always be on the watch.

The next morning, the sun was low in the sky, and the temperature was a bit warmer. The boat had created a deep hollow in the plant when it landed, and the surrounding flesh was still cool to the touch.

"In a few hours, that sun will be almost directly overhead," Forbee-X said, scanning the sky. "The air temperature will rise quickly. Watch."

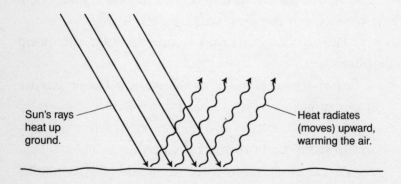

Sun's rays heat up ground.

Heat radiates (moves) upward, warming the air.

Stuart wasn't really paying attention, though. He had noticed a low buzzing noise, and climbed out of the grounded boat to investigate.

The wide crack in the large succulent plant seemed to have come alive. It wriggled and writhed like a wide, black snake, but it wasn't getting anywhere. Stuart swallowed hard and took a few more steps. As he moved closer, one end of the snake seemed to rear up and somehow scatter into the air. Stuart felt something land on his arm. He looked down and saw a black winged insect the size of his palm. It lit for a moment, then flew back toward the plant.

"It's an attack!" Stuart shouted, running toward the plant. He swatted at the huge insects. One by one they hovered overhead for a moment, then dove at the plant again.

Forbee-X and the other droids were there in a nanosecond.

"Where's the attack?" asked Threepio, looking nervously around.

"These insects!" Stuart shouted between swats. "They're going to kill this plant. Don't just stand there, help!"

Forbee-X's screen flashed an unhappy color. "Stuart, I'm afraid it's too late," she said. "This plant's skin is tough, but our crash landing ripped it badly. The thick skin helped the plant keep water in and hungry insects out. Now that the skin is so seriously damaged, it can't do either. The plant will no doubt die."

Stuart gloomily regarded the long tear. The insects were already flying away. Stuart swatted at one last insect, then gave up. "Now it's nothing but insect food. What a waste."

Artoo whistled softly.

"Exactly right, Artoo," Forbee-X said, laying a gentle arm on Stuart's shoulder. "It's not a waste to those insects who feed on it. Or the larger animals who will feed on the insects. This plant is part of a food web. If animal life on this planet is typical, the food web may look something like this."

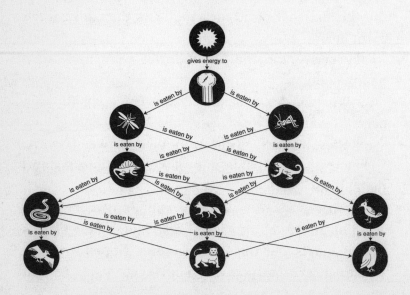

"The death of this one plant will nourish many other animals," Forbee-X concluded.

"Hey, the lizard woke up!" Stuart reached into his jacket and carefully slipped the lizard out. It flicked a long, lazy tongue. "Hey there, buddy," Stuart crooned. "Hungry?"

Stuart broke off a tiny piece of fruit and held it out. The lizard bit the fruit, chewed, then spit out the remainder.

"He's extracting water from it," Forbee-X said approvingly.

"So if we stepped inside, the skin of the plant could insulate us right now?" Stuart asked.

"Exactly right, Stuart," Forbee-X declared. "Isn't it fascinating how nature can protect us? Evaporation would also help us. Water from the plant tissue is turning from a liquid into a gas. For water to evaporate, it needs extra heat energy. In this case, the evaporating water is taking heat energy from the air. And less heat energy means . . ." Forbee-X waited expectantly for Stuart to finish her sentence, her screen sparkling an encouraging blue.

". . . that we would stay cooler!" Stuart finished triumphantly. Then he had another question.

"But there's so much hot air out there," Stuart continued. "Why wouldn't it sink down into the tear in the plant's skin and push the cold air away?"

"Hot air is less dense than cold air," Forbee-X answered. "In general, cold air tends to sink, while hot air rises." Her screen shot a golden light. "Isn't nature marvelous?"

Suddenly, Stuart's mouth dropped open. He looked up at the sky. Then he looked at the parachute. He looked back up at the sky.

"Hot air rises!" he exclaimed. "Of course! I know how to get us out of here!"

AIR TRAVEL

Stuart scrambled back to the boat. He brought back the stove Artoo had fashioned. He pointed from the parachute to the stove to the sky above.

"Is this some kind of game?" Threepio asked. "Because I'm stumped."

"A hot air balloon!" Stuart cried. "We have everything we need. We can make the parachute into a balloon. And we have the stove, and fuel. The boat can carry us."

Forbee-X's screen flashed a rainbow of colors as a stream of data ran across it. Then it cleared and shone bright blue. "I think it might be possible!" she said excitedly.

Artoo beeped a question.

"Artoo just pointed out that we'll have to use all our remaining fuel," Forbee-X translated.

"And he asked if we're willing to take that chance," Threepio rushed in to complete.

"We've got to," Stuart declared. "We don't have much time left."

"Twenty-five hours," Forbee-X confirmed.

"Let's take a vote," Stuart suggested. His hand shot up in the air. "I vote yes."

Forbee-X raised a long metal arm. "I think we ought to take the chance as well."

Artoo beeped in agreement. Everyone looked at Threepio. It wasn't as though he wanted to put his faith in a piece of fabric and a makeshift stove, but he didn't want to stay in a desert, either. He could feel sand gathering in his joint connectors. Besides, if they didn't reach the Rebels in time, he could be stranded on this dreadful planet forever!

He raised his hand. "Let's proceed."

The circuits of Forbee-X and Artoo began to click in happy unison as they made a series of calculations. The two of them sometimes spoke a language Threepio didn't understand, full of numbers and formulas. He was glad to have two smart friends, but sometimes it made him feel lonely.

"What are you talking about, guys?" Stuart asked impatiently.

"We're just planning how to do this," Forbee-X told him. "Luckily, it's not complicated. A hot air balloon needs three basic things."

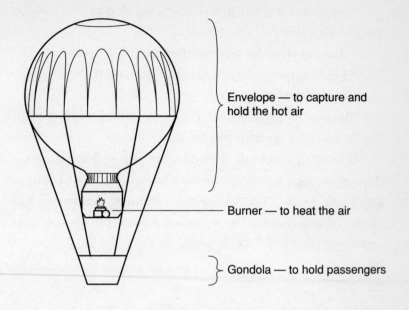

Envelope — to capture and
hold the hot air

Burner — to heat the air

Gondola — to hold passengers

"The burner heats the air inside the envelope,"
Forbee-X continued. "Heated air is less dense than
the cooler air around it. So it rises — or floats upward."

"Where are the steering controls?" Stuart asked.

"There are no controls," Forbee-X answered.
"Other than the burner itself. It allows the pilot to
take the balloon up and down. As I mentioned, to
send the balloon up, you heat the air inside the envelope. To take the balloon back down, you open a vent

at the top of the balloon. The vent allows some hot air to escape, and some cooler air to seep in from below. That makes the balloon denser, so it starts to sink back down toward the ground."

"Up and down?" Stuart frowned. "We have to do more than go *up*. That will just give us a bird's-eye view of the desert."

"I think I've had enough of a bird's-eye view, thank you," Threepio put in.

Forbee-X's screen flashed a sunny yellow for an instant, which meant she was amused. "True, Threepio," she said. "But there is something we need up there. Wind. Actually, we need layers of wind currents — streams of air flowing in different directions. We must find one that will push us south, toward the settlement."

"So how do we find it?" Stuart asked.

"We go up and down until we find the right current," Forbee-X explained. "For instance, the air currents above us could run something like this."

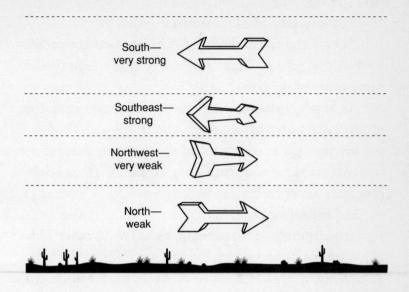

South—
very strong

Southeast—
strong

Northwest—
very weak

North—
weak

In a few hours, they had fashioned the hot air balloon. Artoo drilled more holes in the scrap metal that had gone through so many transformations. Now it would serve as the balloon's "gondola." Threepio made sure there were no holes in the fabric of the parachute, and then, together with Forbee-X, he fastened it to the gondola. Meanwhile, Stuart tied ropes at all four sides of the gondola and staked them into the sand.

Artoo propped the stove above the center of the

gondola, and they loaded the supplies. Then, Artoo started up the stove and they carefully filled the balloon with hot air.

"It's going to work!" Stuart crowed.

"It looks a little makeshift," Threepio said critically.

"As long as it flies," Forbee-X said. "That's the important thing. Let's board!"

Forbee-X, Artoo, and Threepio stepped into the gondola. One by one, Stuart cut the lines. Then he quickly jumped in as the gondola began to rise.

"Artoo, are you sure this is going to work?" Threepio whispered.

Artoo beeped cheerfully.

"You *think* so?" Threepio asked in a panic. He squeezed his photoreceptors shut.

"What a view!" Forbee-X exclaimed a moment later.

"Totally galactic!" Stuart cried.

Cautiously, Threepio reactivated his photoreceptors. It was good to see the burning desert below, and not be in the middle of it.

"We're going a little too fast, I think," Forbee-X said to Artoo, who was controlling their ascent. "Stuart might run into problems."

"What problems?" Stuart asked gleefully. "This is the way to travel!"

Stuart sounded breathless. Threepio guessed he was excited. But then Stuart began to take in breath with great gasps. His eyes widened in panic as he fought to breathe.

"The atmosphere is too thin, Artoo!" Forbee-X rapped out. "Bring us down!"

As Artoo guided them down, Forbee-X turned to Stuart.

"Don't worry, Stuart. You'll feel better in a minute. The atmosphere is thinner the higher we go. That means that the air molecules are farther apart. Each breath has fewer molecules in it."

"So I had to breathe harder to get more molecules," Stuart guessed. "I sure didn't like the feeling."

"No, it must be unpleasant," Forbee-X said. "We have to be careful not to get so high again."

Artoo gave a happy beep.

"Artoo says we've found a good wind current. It's bringing us southward," Threepio explained.

Stuart turned to face forward. The wind blew his dark hair away from his face as he stared at the horizon. "I'm coming, Father," he whispered.

They traveled over desert and forest and plain as the day went on. The sun set, and the sky twinkled with stars. While Stuart slept close to the stove for warmth, his hand resting on the lizard underneath his jacket, Artoo, Threepio, and Forbee-X kept the balloon on course.

Stuart awakened with the sunrise. He munched on a protein cube and a piece of fruit as the sky turned blood-red. The color streaked through a bank of dark clouds.

"What beautiful colors!" Threepio exclaimed. "I'm sure it's a good omen."

Forbee-X's screen went gray. "I'm afraid it isn't, Threepio," she said in a worried tone. "I don't like the shape of those clouds."

"I think they're rather pretty," Threepio said, admiring them.

"Look how some of them spread out on top," Stuart agreed as he fed a piece of fruit to the lizard. "Like a Wookiee on a bad hair day."

"That one looks more like a Fuzzum to me," Threepio said, pointing.

As Stuart laughed, Forbee-X's screen flashed a warning red. "What I see are cumulonimbus clouds with anvil-shaped tops."

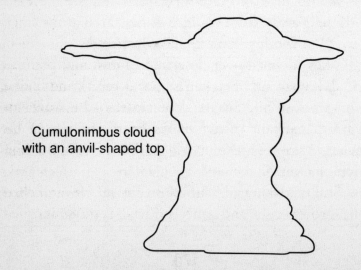

Cumulonimbus cloud
with an anvil-shaped top

"Okay, so it's not a mussed-up Wookiee," Stuart said, still grinning. "But what's the problem?"

"Clouds are made mostly of water droplets and water vapor — water that has evaporated into gas," Forbee-X explained. "Because those clouds reach so high in the air, they're super cold inside. In those chilly temperatures, some of the water vapor in the clouds has turned into ice crystals. Some of the water drops have frozen into tiny ice pellets called graupel. Fierce winds blowing up and down inside the cloud toss the crystals and graupel around. When the two kinds of ice collide, they sometimes become charged with static electricity. The crystals become positively charged and the graupel becomes negatively charged."

"I know what static electricity is," Stuart said. "Back home, when I walk across my bedroom carpet, I get charged with it. Then, if I touch metal, I feel a little shock. It's no big deal. Why should it be a problem inside the cloud?"

"If the ice crystals and graupel stayed mixed together, it wouldn't be," Forbee-X answered. "But the cloud has strong upward and downward winds called updrafts and downdrafts. Because the ice crystals are lighter, many of them are blown to the top of the cloud. That gives the upper part of the cloud a positive charge. Meanwhile, the heavier graupel sinks toward the bottom of the cloud. So the lower part of the cloud becomes negatively charged, like this."

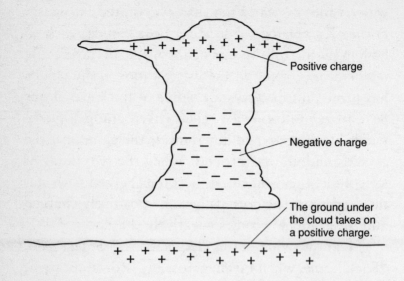

Positive charge

Negative charge

The ground under the cloud takes on a positive charge.

Stuart pointed at the screen. "All this built up positive and negative charge must make for a huge discharge. That sounds almost like —"

Suddenly, a huge flash lit the sky.

"Lightning," Stuart finished. He tucked the lizard back into the sling.

Forbee confirmed Stuart's conclusion with a new diagram.

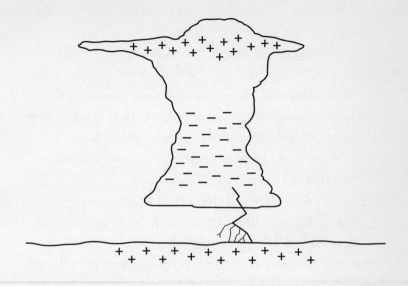

"Artoo, I suggest we land immediately," Forbee-X said urgently. "The land looks green below. We should be able to find shelter."

Artoo began a slow descent. But they were caught by a fierce wind current, which blew them directly into the course of the storm. Lightning flashed and the skies opened. Rain drenched them within seconds. The gondola swung crazily with the force of the winds. Artoo battled to keep them on course, but he had enough trouble keeping them from overturning.

"We've got to land!" Forbee-X shouted.

Artoo whistled at Threepio.

"All right, Artoo," Threepio yelled over a thunderclap. "We'll guide you down!"

The three of them peered over the side while Artoo handled the descent. The rain created a gray curtain that made it impossible to see clearly. Stuart wiped his eyes constantly, trying to peer downward. Threepio thought he spied a green field below.

"There!" he cried, pointing.

"That looks perfect!" Forbee-X agreed. "Just about a hundred feet to the left, Artoo!"

The wind gust blew them over the field.

"Down!" Threepio shouted.

Artoo piloted the balloon down to the planet's surface. The gondola bumped gently on the ground.

"Good work!" Threepio congratulated him. "We're safe!"

Just as he said this, a fierce gust of wind knocked over the gondola. They spilled out. But instead of landing on the ground, they crashed right through it!

A LONG WAY DOWN

To Threepio's surprise, the green "field" turned out to be a thick blanket of treetops. He hit a branch and bounced, then fell a few feet to bounce on another.

"Ow!" He heard Stuart below him, also bouncing from branch to branch. Artoo clunked his way downward, beeping wildly. Forbee-X's circuits clicked and her screen flashed red with each jarring collision.

The final drop was onto a carpet of thick moss. Threepio landed with a bump.

He sorrowfully regarded a dent in his right flank. "My poor metal! Stuart, are you all right? Artoo? Forbee?"

Artoo beeped a weak reply, and Forbee-X's screen flashed slowly from color to color as she checked her circuits. "I'm fine," she said.

Stuart flexed his arms and legs. "Nothing's broken. But I lost the lizard!"

"Oh, that's too bad," Threepio said politely.

"Don't worry, Stuart. The lizard has wings, remember?" Forbee-X said. "It probably flew away in the confusion. It's very warm here. I'd say we're in its native habitat."

"It *is* warm," Stuart noted. "But it's morning. Shouldn't it be winter?"

"I believe that we're close to the planet's equator — the imaginary line that divides the planet's northern hemisphere from its southern hemisphere," Forbee-X said. "Let me show you."

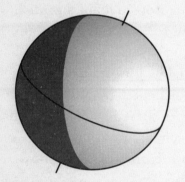
Northern summer

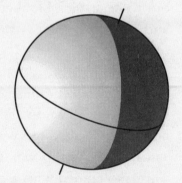
Northern winter

Sunlight is always fairly strong near the equator. As a result, areas near the equator don't have the four seasons we have been experiencing.

"The bad news is, we were blown too far south by the storm," Forbee-X continued. "We've overshot the city."

"Oh, I knew there would be bad news," Threepio moaned. "So what do we do now?"

Artoo beeped a suggestion.

"Climb back *up*?" Threepio asked in disbelief. "I barely made it down alive!"

Forbee-X listened to Artoo's chirps and whirrs. "He's right," she told the others. "We need the supplies. And we might be able to salvage the parachute. We only have twelve hours left to find the city."

"I'll go and check it out," Stuart offered.

"Excellent suggestion!" Threepio agreed. He settled himself against the trunk.

"I think we should all go," Forbee-X said. "If we can't salvage the parachute, we'll have to get the supplies down anyway. We all have to pitch in."

The branches were wide and spaced close together. Stuart nimbly hoisted himself from branch to branch, but Artoo often needed help. At last they reached the large branch where the gondola had landed. It was wedged in the V where the branch met the tree.

Artoo examined the parachute while Forbee-X, Stuart, and Threepio checked the supplies.

Artoo gave an unhappy series of beeps.

"We can't use it?" Threepio sighed. "We lost most of the supplies, too."

"We've got to find a way out of here!" Stuart said anxiously. "Time is running out!"

"Well, it could be worse," Forbee-X said.

"I can't imagine how," Threepio said. "Well, I suppose I *can*. But I certainly don't want to."

"At least we're in no immediate danger," Forbee-X pointed out. "Let's put our heads together and try to figure out the next —"

Forbee-X stopped abruptly. Her auditory sensors rose and trembled as they took a reading. "Do you hear it?" she whispered.

Everyone listened carefully. Threepio heard it first — the *caw caw* that sent his circuits into a tizzy. "Not those birds!" he cried.

"Let's not panic," Forbee-X said. "We're well concealed by the branches. And the lizard isn't here to alert them to our presence."

Just then, Threepio saw a green flash. The lizard flew down and landed on Stuart's shoulder.

"Hey there!" Stuart greeted it happily.

The lizard opened its mouth and screeched. Stuart quickly clamped his hand around the lizard's mouth. But another, louder screech followed the first one.

"Stuart, keep it quiet!" Threepio warned.

"I'm trying!" Stuart protested.

Another screech rose in the forest. Then another, and another. Threepio looked around wildly. Now he could see that lizards surrounded them, sitting on branches and blending in with the greenery. Their mouths were open as the screeching noises grew louder and louder.

As the birds came closer, the screeching of the lizards intensified, causing Stuart to put his hands over his ears. Above them, the birds began to circle as their numbers grew. A bloodthirsty *caw caw* echoed through the forest.

"Go ahead and say it, Threepio," Stuart whispered. "We're doomed."

UNDER ATTACK

Artoo beeped rapidly and flashed his lights.

"The gondola!" Threepio cried.

"We should flip it over —" Forbee-X started.

"— and use it for protection —" Threepio said.

"— with Stuart on the bottom again," Forbee-X concluded.

With a mighty pull, Threepio loosened the gondola from the V of the trunk. With Stuart and Forbee-X's help, he flipped it over. The lizard took off, and Stuart crawled underneath. The droids followed. Threepio peeked out from the small crack left at the bottom.

"More and more lizards are flying in to join the others," he whispered. "It looks as though the whole forest is alive."

"I can hear them," Stuart said, wincing.

"The screeching is a distress call," Forbee-X murmured. "When Stuart's lizard made it during our first encounter, he was out of his habitat, so none of his fellow creatures could answer."

The shadow of the birds' giant wings fell over the forest. Their great *caws* filled the air. "They're here," Threepio whispered.

But this time, the bloodcurdling cries were answered by the screeching of the lizards.

"What's happening?" Stuart asked.

"I think the birds are confused by the number of lizards," Threepio said excitedly. "They're just circling. Now the lizards are taking off! They're attacking the birds!"

Threepio tilted the boat so that he could monitor the bloodthirsty battle. The lizards flew toward the circling birds in close formation. Then, at the last moment, two sections separated at both ends of the line and dove toward the birds.

"It's a double flanking maneuver!" Threepio cried. "Oh, Master Luke would be so impressed!"

The great battle began. The birds were larger and stronger, but the lizards were more numerous, and had better tactics. They encircled the birds in a pincer movement and attacked them ferociously. Sunlight flashed on iridescent skin as their claws and teeth ripped into the cawing birds.

With flapping winds and angry cries, each bird tried vainly to peck at their smaller attackers. But the lizards hung on, shredding flesh with their sharp teeth and digging their claws into the wings of the frantic birds.

With dying cries, one bird fell to the forest floor. Then another. Their comrades tried to wheel and launch an attack on the lizards, but they were outmaneuvered once more. Again and again the lizards dove relentlessly at the bloodied birds, tearing into their flesh and then flying off, only to return and assault them again.

With a huge, angry cry, one bird took off, calling for the others to follow. With shredded flesh and tattered feathers, the flock made a disorderly retreat.

"The birds are leaving!" Threepio cried. "We're saved!"

Threepio pushed the gondola over. They climbed out just in time to see the last ragged birds flying away as fast as they could. The lizards slowly dropped back to the shelter of the trees. One of the lizards separated from the pack and flew to Stuart. It perched on his shoulder.

"Thank you, fella," Stuart told it. "That was a hypergalactic save!"

Threepio climbed back into the right-side-up gondola. He sighed. "Now what?"

Artoo trundled over to sit next to him. Forbee-X followed, and then Stuart, still petting the lizard.

Artoo whistled and chirped.

"Artoo thinks we should abandon the gondola and hike out," Threepio translated. "We can forage for food for Stuart on the way."

"That could be an unacceptable risk," Forbee-X said, her screen dimming. "Perhaps we should try to fix the parachute first."

"Oh, dear." Threepio sighed. "I don't know what the right thing to do is."

The lizard croaked in Stuart's ear.

"He's trying to tell us something," Stuart said excitedly as the croaking grew louder.

"Sorry," Threepio said. "I speak six million languages, but Flying Lizard isn't one of them."

Suddenly, the lizards in the surrounding trees took to the air. In a mass, they flew toward the group.

"They're attacking!" Threepio cried.

But the lizards didn't touch Stuart or the droids. With their powerful jaws, they grabbed hold of the ropes that had once fastened the parachute to the gondola. They flapped their wings, and the gondola slowly rose in the air.

"They're helping us!" Stuart cried. "He's thanking us for bringing him home, I bet."

"It's a good assumption, Stuart," Forbee-X agreed

as the gondola moved smoothly into the air. Soon, they were gliding above the trees.

"We're moving north," Forbee-X noted. "They must know where we were headed. These lizards must have a superior form of intelligence, even if they can't communicate. They must have figured we want to go back to our own kind."

"I knew it," Stuart said.

They soared just above the treetops. The only sound was the soft whisper of the lizards' wings. The sound lulled the passengers, and Stuart grew drowsy. Soon, the forest was left behind and they skimmed above a flat, arid plain.

"I see it!" Threepio suddenly called. "I see the city!"

Stuart woke. He craned his neck. "I see it, too!" he cried excitedly. "It has some sort of dome over it."

"An enclosed city," Forbee-X said, nodding. "That makes sense, considering the climate extremes."

"What's the time check, Forbee?" Stuart asked anxiously.

"We have a little over two hours to reach the city and locate the Rebel faction," Forbee-X said. "Not much time."

"It will have to be enough," Stuart said grimly.

The lizards' wings beat slowly, as if drawing the gondola was becoming more of an effort. Stuart felt the skin of his little friend.

"He's getting cold, Forbee," he said worriedly.

"We're too far north, out of their habitat," Forbee-X said. "Since they're cold-blooded, they're slowing down. They have to return."

"Did you hear that, fella?" Stuart told the lizard. "You've done all you can."

The lizard gave a soft croak. The lizards carrying the gondola stopped struggling. They glided softly down to the planet's surface.

"Thank you," Stuart told the lizard. Artoo flashed his lights. Forbee-X's screen glowed her prettiest rainbow. Threepio bowed.

"We wish you a safe journey home," he said.

The lizard rubbed its head against Stuart's shoulder. Then, with a final soft cry, the small creature flapped its wings and rose. Together with the rest of the flock, it flew southward. Stuart waved until the last lizard was out of sight.

The sun was now low in the sky. Clouds rolled in from the west. The sky was an odd greenish color. Forbee-X eyed it uneasily. Data flowed across her screen.

"We'd better start walking," Stuart said. "How long do you think it will take to reach the city, Forbee?"

"I'm not sure," Forbee-X replied. "I just hope the weather holds."

Just then, they heard a rumble of thunder.

"So we get a little wet," Stuart said with a shrug. "We've been through worse."

Forbee-X eyed the clouds anxiously. She pointed to a funnel-shaped cloud in the distance. "Welcome to worse," she said.

TWIST AND SHOUT

"What is it, Forbee?" Threepio asked over Artoo's inquisitive beep. He eyed the cloud nervously.

"That funnel-shaped cloud is produced by a tube of whirling wind called a tornado," Forbee-X said. Her screen flashed rapidly.

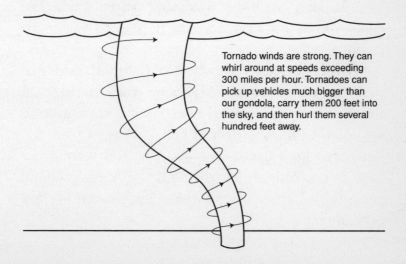

Tornado winds are strong. They can whirl around at speeds exceeding 300 miles per hour. Tornadoes can pick up vehicles much bigger than our gondola, carry them 200 feet into the sky, and then hurl them several hundred feet away.

"If a tornado can carry a gondola," Threepio said hesitantly, "does that mean it could carry *us*?"

"I'm afraid so," Forbee-X said. "We must find shelter!"

Artoo rotated his domed head. Forbee-X's head spun around. Threepio and Stuart craned their necks. All they saw was flat, empty plain.

"The safest place is underground," Forbee-X explained. "Even a deep ditch would help."

"Maybe we can dig one with the gondola," Threepio suggested.

"No time," Forbee-X's voice rose over the sound of the rising wind.

"Let's strap ourselves in the gondola," Stuart suggested.

"I'm afraid that won't do much good," Forbee-X said reluctantly.

"At least we'll be together," Stuart said. The wind tore at his clothing, and he had to yell to be heard.

Forbee-X nodded slowly. "All right," she shouted over the rising wind. "My outer shell is made of shock-absorbing material. Keep your arms around me, Stuart. I'll try to protect you."

They climbed into the gondola and wound the spun carbon rope around themselves. Forbee-X wound her legs and arms around Stuart and locked her fingers and toes.

The sound of the wind was terrifying. A gust snatched the remaining supplies out from the bottom, and they were carried away. There was no time to worry about them. The wind was a screaming force now, blowing the gondola horizontally straight toward the funnel cloud. A whirling column of sand — the tornado! — rose before them.

"Hold on!" Forbee-X yelled over the screaming wind. "We're being sucked in!"

It was a sound louder than anything Threepio had ever heard. Louder than the sound of a fleet of X-wings taking off. Louder than a Star Destroyer firing all of its laser cannons at once.

The wind tore at the gondola, driving it upward into the tornado. The gondola spun slowly at first, then picked up speed as it rose. The world became a blur of flying dust and roaring wind. Threepio could only lock his fingers around the gondola and hang on, his visual sensors closed tight.

It seemed to last forever, but it was probably no more than seconds before they spun out of the funnel. They flew through the air and landed with a crash.

"Stuart? Master Stuart!" Threepio cried. Stuart's head was still pillowed against Forbee-X.

"Stuart!" Forbee-X called frantically. "Are you all right?"

Slowly, Stuart raised his head. He blinked his green eyes. "Hypergalactic," he said shakily.

"Oh, dear. You gave me such a fright," Threepio scolded. "I'm glad to see you're all right. As for me, a few more dents don't matter, I suppose."

"That landing was softer than I expected," Forbee-X said. "What exactly did we land *on*?"

They peered over the gondola's edge.

"It looks like some sort of dried grass," Threepio observed.

Artoo chirped and whirred.

Threepio surveyed their immediate surroundings. "Yes, Artoo. I see those heaps of grass over there. Each one seems to have a conical shape. Almost like a —"

"Roof," Stuart supplied. "But it's not attached to a house."

"In tornado country, people often build shelters underground," Forbee-X observed. "If this area is populated, those could be shelters. Which is good for us, since conditions are still ripe for another twister. I suggest that we locate the openings to the shelters. Maybe we can find people to convey us to the city."

"Oh, dear. I think they found *us*," Threepio said.

Around them, openings in the grassy mounds began to appear. Doors in the mounds lifted, and people began to climb out. They carried sharp pronged blades on top of slender sticks, and wore several weapon-filled belts around their tunics.

The settlers circled the droids and Stuart. Some-one pointed to the damage to the grassy mound where the gondola had landed. The settlers began complaining in a strange, harsh language.

"They don't look too happy," Stuart muttered.

"Yes," Forbee-X remarked. "It appears we are in a tight spot."

"No kidding," Stuart said, eyeing the fierce-looking group. "I say we take them. If we don't get out of here now, we'll never be rescued."

"I suggest —" Threepio began, but was interrupted by Artoo's beeps.

"Artoo says we have the element of surprise," Forbee-X translated. "That's true."

Frustration washed over Threepio. As usual, no one was asking his opinion! "What I think —"

"On the count of three," Stuart said out of the corner of his mouth. "One, two —"

"Hang on, Stuart," Forbee-X whispered. "We haven't heard from Threepio."

Gratified, Threepio spoke in a low tone. "I suggest we apologize. After all, we did wreck their dwelling. And may I point out that I'm programmed for diplomacy in six million lang —"

Suddenly, a bearded cave dweller jumped forward. He shook his pronged spear angrily and let loose a flood of language. Threepio's circuits clicked as his memory banks attempted to identify the language. He located words and phrases, then recognized the language as N'or. This meant he was able to translate what the stranger was saying.

"Oh, dear," Threepio whispered to his friends. "I'm afraid they're very, very angry."

"So let's charge!" Stuart suggested.

"Let me try diplomacy first," Threepio suggested. He knew from the N'or vocabulary that the population was inclined to use flowery phrases for apology and flattery.

Threepio stood. He held out his arms, palms out. "Strangers and friends, we apologize with all our hearts for landing on your dwelling. The tornado picked us up and dropped us here. Not for twelve thousand moons will I ever allow myself to forgive this terrible event." Then he bowed his head.

There was a murmur from the group. Threepio heard a woman say "appropriate sentiment." Perhaps he had saved them from punishment!

"We should forgive them, perhaps," a man muttered. "The whirlwind has done similar damage. No one can predict how it will move."

Just as Threepio began to relax, the man with the glistening black beard stepped forward. Threepio noted anxiously that he was tall and muscular. He looked like a leader.

"I do not trust these strangers who dropped from

the sky," the settler said in a deep voice. "I think the golden being is lying!"

The cave dwellers looked at one another. "Granit is usually correct," someone murmured.

"Our apologies are weak compared to the damage," Threepio said quickly. "But we would commit ourselves to repairing the dwelling."

"Easy for him to say," Granit snorted. "They do not look as though they could fix a child's toy."

The cave dwellers moved forward. Threepio noted nervously that their hands went to their belts, casually moving for their weapons.

"Threepio?" Stuart asked nervously.

"Give me that azurite you stole on Yavin 4," Threepio said urgently.

"But I gave it back," Stuart protested.

"Give it to me, Master Stuart," Threepio ordered. "I know you saved a piece and it's in your pocket. It's our last hope."

Artoo beeped, and Forbee-X's screen flashed. "Do it, Stuart," she ordered crisply.

Stuart dug into his pocket and handed Threepio the azurite.

"We suggest a game of chance of your choosing," Threepio said. "If we win, you will help us reach the domed city. If we lose, we will give you our most valuable possession."

Threepio held the chunk of azurite aloft. The setting sun hit the mineral, causing it to flash with a clear blue light. Azurite was renowned as one of the most beautiful minerals in any system.

"We accept your offer and suggest space poker," Granit said.

"Agreed," Threepio said.

"The azurite is not enough, however," Granit said. "It is hardly worth the destruction of our meeting house. It took us months to build it."

"That is true," someone said. "But what else should we ask for?"

"I say after we win, we dismantle the droids and sell them for scrap," a woman suggested.

"Oh, dear," Threepio murmured.

"And kill the boy," someone added. "Why should we feed him? There is little enough to go around."

"That is foolish waste," another woman said. "We should sell them all to the next slaver who comes around."

Everyone nodded at this.

"What are they saying?" Stuart asked Threepio.

Threepio instantly decided it was better not to tell the others the grisly fate that awaited them if they lost. After all, it was still possible they could win the game of chance.

"They have decided on space poker. I have one suggestion," Threepio said. He turned to Forbee-X. "Don't lose."

ODDS AGAINST

"Space poker?" Stuart exclaimed. "That's my game!"

"But Forbee-X can calculate odds and strategies," Threepio protested. "She should play."

"Poker isn't about knowing the odds," Stuart declared. "It's about playing *against* them. I haven't met my match yet."

"I confess that I don't feel confident about my abilities in this area," Forbee-X said. "Perhaps we should let Stuart try."

Artoo whistled agreement. Threepio nodded reluctantly, and the four of them followed Granit to his cavelike dwelling.

Stuart and Granit sat across from each other at a small round table. Granit dealt out a series of cards marked with basic symbols. Threepio didn't understand the game, and he didn't want to try. He just had to trust Stuart.

Stuart studied his hand while Granit did the same.

Forbee-X inched over to Threepio's side. "Congratulations, Threepio. It would have been terrible to come so far only to be captured or dismantled. If we make it out of here soon, we might be able to make it to the city in time. How did you know to wager the azurite?"

"It was fairly simple," Threepio whispered back. "I guessed the cave dwellers were devoted to games of chance when I scanned their vocabulary. There were many expressions that had to do with betting and odds. I also saw that they wore laser dice hanging on their belts."

"I see," Forbee-X said, nodding. "They most likely gamble as a way to pass the time during the many retreats they must make underground. Excellent deduction. We couldn't have done it without you," she whispered as Stuart slapped down a card.

Artoo softly whistled his agreement. Granit played a card, and Stuart studied his hand.

"I just hope Stuart is able to win," Threepio added in a murmur to Forbee-X.

"Well, if he doesn't, we're just out a chunk of azurite," Forbee-X answered philosophically.

Threepio gulped. He didn't want to mention that the stakes were much higher.

He turned back to Granit and Stuart. He couldn't tell who was winning and who was losing. Stuart held his cards and regarded them with a face carved in stone. Granit whistled under his breath in a careless way.

"Two turbos," Stuart said. "Down easy."

"One propulsion," Granit said. "Over and down."

Threepio had no idea what that meant. But Stuart looked confident, so that gave him hope. Unless Stuart was bluffing. Threepio grew nervous again.

Granit squinted at Stuart as Stuart lay down a card. Then, he laughed. Threepio did not like the sound of the laugh. Not at all.

Granit threw down his cards. Stuart did the same. "Full planetary system," Granit said in a satisfied tone, using Stuart's language instead of his native N'or. "That beats three satellites any day."

"What does that mean?" Threepio asked nervously.

"It means I lost," Stuart said, dejected. "Give him the azurite, Threepio. Then let's get out of here."

Granit held out his beefy hand. Threepio placed the azurite in his palm. A second later, it disappeared into the pocket of his tunic.

"And now, the fun begins," Granit said. He reached into a dark corner and withdrew a long, sharp weapon.

Threepio took a step backward as he was struck

dumb with fear. He recognized the weapon as a force pike, a pole arm tipped with a vibro-edged head that could kill or stun with a single touch. The force pike was the weapon of choice of the Emperor's Royal Guard.

Artoo gave a soft, warning beep. Forbee-X's screen rapidly flashed red.

"What's going on, Granit?" Stuart asked, edging next to the droids. "We had a deal. You got your azurite."

"Didn't your friend tell you?" Granit asked. "Now you are our slaves."

"Uh, Threepio? D-did you leave something out?" Stuart stammered, backing away from the tip of the force pike.

Granit leaned close to them. His black gaze was fierce and ruthless. Threepio shrank back in fear. What would he do? Destroy them? Sell them to a slave trader?

"Looks like the Force wasn't with you today, Stuie," Granit said. He winked. "The princess will probably tell you not to gamble so much in the future."

"The p-princess?" Threepio stammered. "You can't be . . ."

"On your side," Granit answered gruffly. "Lucky for you." He shook the force pike. "I got this off an Imperial during a Rebel skirmish on Romm. Princess

Leia contacted me and told me to be on the lookout for three droids and a small boy. My orders are to transport you off the planet."

Artoo beeped a question, and Threepio translated. "What exactly *is* this planet? Are we still in the Delantine system?"

Granit nodded. "This is the planet Da'nor. Unfortunately, the Imperials have taken over. Rebel operatives have all transported off the planet. My orders were to stay behind and wait for you four."

"So the domed city isn't safe," Threepio said. "Oh, dear."

"You're lucky you didn't reach it," Granit told them. "You would have been arrested immediately. The Imperials are conducting surprise searches of all the camps around the city like this one. Every moment you're here puts you in danger."

"Can you arrange to get us back to Yavin 4?" Threepio asked hopefully.

"Sorry," Granit said shortly. "Our ships on Da'nor no longer have that range. The Imperials have removed all hyperspace controls to keep us local and within their control."

Artoo whirred and beeped.

"Do you have the range to send us to a port that *isn't* under Imperial control?" Threepio translated.

Granit shook his head. "The best I can do is bring you to the secret Rebel base on Romm."

"But the Princess ordered evacuation of the entire Delantine system," Forbee-X pointed out.

"Officially, yes," Granit admitted. "But one faction remains to help coordinate an overthrow of the Imperials. It's not an easy journey. Imperial troops and spies are reported to be everywhere."

"That sounds dangerous," Threepio remarked nervously.

"Staying here would be more so," Granit told them grimly.

"But Romm is exactly where we want to go!" Stuart said excitedly. "My father has been captured. We can form a rescue party on Romm."

Granit frowned. "Princess Leia didn't say anything about a rescue party."

"I suggest we deal with one thing at a time," Forbee-X said. "If Granit is correct, we must leave Da'nor as quickly as possible."

"Excuse me, Granit," Threepio said politely. "Would you mind if we talked it over privately? We all have to agree on decisions."

"Of course." Granit bowed and retreated out of his dwelling.

As soon as the door closed behind him, Threepio turned to the others worriedly. "How do we know we can trust Granit?" he asked. "He could be lying about the last Rebel faction on Romm. What if he's really an Imperial? After all, he has a force pike!"

"I read him as sincere," Forbee-X said.

Artoo beeped agreement.

"I don't think we have a choice," Stuart said. "We have to trust him."

"We can't stay here," Forbee-X pointed out. They all turned to Threepio.

"Oh, all right," Threepio agreed fretfully. "We'll go with Granit. But don't blame me if we get into another dreadful adventure!"

STAR WARS SCIENCE ACTIVITIES
Experiments for your own world

1. Hot Air Power

When Stuart and the droids escaped the desert in a balloon, they used rising hot air to get off the ground. Can you harness this power in your own room? Give this activity a spin to find out.

Materials

notebook paper
pen
scissors
thread (heavier string won't work)
paper clip
table lamp (with a shade) or desk lamp

It must have a regular incandescent bulb. A fluorescent bulb won't work. If you use a desk lamp, turn it upside down so that the bulb points up.

1. Trace the pattern on the next page onto notebook paper.
2. Cut along the curving line to make a spiral.
3. Use a pen to poke a small hole through the dot. Tie a piece of thread to a paper clip. Push the other

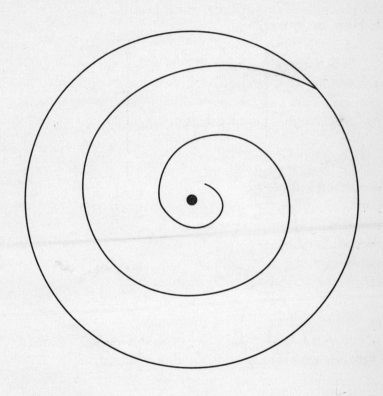

end of the thread through the hole. Hold the thread so that the paper spiral dangles.

4. Close any open windows and turn off any fans. Hold the spiral over an unlit lamp. (See diagram below.) The spiral may turn for a minute if the thread is twisted. Wait until the spiral is still.

5. Turn on the lamp. Wait a few seconds. What happens?

The lit bulb warms the air around it. That makes the air less dense than the other air in the room. The heated air rises, turning the spiral as it goes.

2. Mouth Lightning

Crunch up some candy to create static electricity — and make some mini-lightning in your own mouth!

Materials

wintergreen candy (like Wint-O-Green Life Savers)
dark room or closet
mirror

1. Read these directions ahead of time, because you're going to have to do this in the dark!

2. Go into an unlit room. Let your eyes get used to the dark.

3. Hold a mirror in front of your face. Put a wintergreen candy between your back teeth. Try to keep it as dry as possible. Bite down on it with your mouth open. Do you see any flashes of light in the mirror?

When you bite into hard candy, your teeth crunch the sugar crystals inside. That makes static electricity, which causes sparks to fly. The sparks themselves aren't bright enough to see. However, they cause some gas molecules in the air to give off ultraviolet, or UV, light. The wintergreen flavoring in the candy absorbs the UV light. That makes the candy glow for a split second.

3. Balloon Thunder

How does lightning make thunder? This balloon experiment is bursting with answers.

Materials

two balloons (use stretchy latex balloons; shiny Mylar balloons won't work)
water
pin

1. Blow up one balloon. Fill the other with water.
2. Hold the air-filled balloon away from you and pop it with a pin. Listen to the sound it makes.

A balloon compresses the air inside it — squeezes it into a smaller space. When you popped your balloon, the air expanded again. Any time air expands quickly, it makes a loud sound.

Thunder works much the same way. As lightning streaks through the sky, it heats the air around it to more than 43,000°F. As the air heats up, it expands superquickly — making the superloud sound we call thunder.

3. Hold the water-filled balloon over a sink and pop it with a pin. Listen to the sound it makes.

A balloon can't compress water very much. So when you pop a water balloon, there isn't nearly as much sound.

4. Tornado in a Jar

Twist up a tiny "tornado" that can fit in the palm of your hand.

Materials

empty plastic jar with lid (it should be about the size of a peanut butter jar)
teaspoon
dishwashing detergent
vinegar
food coloring

1. Fill the empty jar two-thirds full of water.
2. Add 1 teaspoon dishwashing detergent.
3. Add 1 teaspoon vinegar.
4. Add 2 drops of food coloring.
5. Replace the lid and tighten it well.
6. Hold the jar from the bottom and swirl it around quickly a few times. Hold it up to a light. (A brightly lit window or computer screen works well.) Watch for a funnel-shaped cloud of bubbles. If you don't see one, swirl the jar again.

The forces that created your "tornado in a jar" are much different than those that produce real tornadoes. However, a funnel-shaped cloud often appears in the center of a tornado. The tornado itself is an invisible tube of fast-whirling wind.

SCIENCE FACTS FOR USE ON EARTH

You Can't Break Newton's Laws:

The Third Law of Motion is known to Earth scientists as Newton's Third Law. Here's a rundown of all three of Newton's laws:

• Newton's First Law of Motion: If no outside forces act on a moving object, it will keep traveling in the same direction and at the same speed. If the object isn't moving at all, it will stay still. Forces include pushes, pulls, friction, and gravity. Almost every object on Earth is under the influence of some of these forces. But an object hurtling through space, far from any planets or stars, is free of them.

• Newton's Second Law of Motion: When you apply a force to an object, its speed and/or direction changes. The change is determined by the amount of force, and its direction. Even if you never heard of this law, you apply it with every move you make. For instance, anyone knows that the harder you hit a baseball, the faster it flies. And where your bat touches the ball helps determine whether you make a line drive or a pop foul.

- Newton's Third Law of Motion: For every force, there is an equal force in the opposite direction.

The Birds and the V's

Many migrating Earth birds, like Canada geese, fly in V-formation just like the birds of Planet X. Scientists think this gives them two advantages, but they aren't sure which is more important:

- Easier flying. As the lead goose flies, it creates an updraft behind each of its wings. Two geese fall in behind the lead bird to take advantage of the updrafts, which makes flying easier. Other geese could follow those two to take advantage of those birds' updrafts, and so on.

- Better communication. To avoid crashes, each goose needs to see the geese around it. Following in a V-formation allows the birds to avoid each other's blind spots. (See diagram on the next page.)

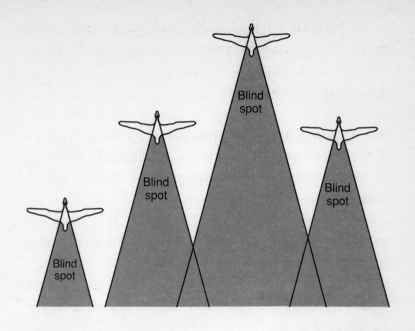

Four Seasons in One Day?

Forbee-X has good reason to doubt the existence of a planet with four seasons between sunrise and sunset. For a planet to circle its sun twice in twenty-four hours, it would have to orbit incredibly close to its sun. Temperatures would reach thousands of degrees Fahrenheit — way too hot for plants or animals to survive. Liquid water would boil away instantly. A planet that close to the sun would also experience "tidal lock" — the same side of the planet would always face the sun. That means there would be no day and night. Instead, half the planet would always have daylight while the other half was always in the dark.

In our solar system, there is one planet that orbits the sun in less than a day — Venus. But a "day" on Venus is about eight Earth months long! (Remember, a planet's day is the time it takes to rotate once on its axis.)

Insulate This!

Different animals use different kinds of insulation to keep themselves warm.

• Polar bears are so well adapted for staying warm that they're more likely to overheat than to get too chilly!

• Since fat makes a great insulator, seals and whales have a thick layer surrounding their bodies. The thick fat keeps their body heat from seeping into the cold ocean waters. Camels, on the other hand, have to endure hot desert days. They don't want a heat-keeping layer of fat. So they pile up their fat in a hump instead.

The Eye of the Storm

On average, more people are killed by lightning in a year than by tornadoes and hurricanes put together. The safest place to be during a lightning storm is inside a house or other building with plumbing or electricity. Stay away from electrical appliances and running water. Hard-topped cars and buses are also safe, especially if you sit away from the sides of the vehicle. However, a close lightning strike could cause an auto accident by damaging a car or startling a driver. So if you're caught on the road during a thunderstorm, it's safest to have the driver pull over until the storm passes.

More people are struck by lightning just before and just after a thunderstorm than during the storm itself. If you see storm clouds approaching, head for safety. And don't head outside again until half an hour after the last lightning flash you see or the last rumbling of thunder you hear.

Tornadoes produce the world's strongest winds. The greatest danger during a tornado is from objects being thrown around by the wind. The safest place to wait out a tornado is somewhere below ground. If no good shelter is available, try to get as low as possible, like in a ditch.